BEAR and SQUIRREL are FRIENDS

are FRIENDS

Yes, Really!

Deb Pilutti

SCHOLASTIC INC.

ISBN 978-1-338-11292-4

12 11 10 9 8 7 6 5 4 3 2   17 18 19 20 21

Printed in the U.S.A.   40

First Scholastic printing, September 2016

Book design by Lizzy Bromley
The text for this book is set in Garamond 3.
The illustrations for this book are rendered in gouache.

for
Hope and Christine

It's true that Bear was much bigger than Squirrel.
And that a bear will *sometimes* eat a squirrel for dinner.
But Bear and Squirrel were friends.
They had a lot in common.

They liked to gather
acorns and blueberries.

Bear was very strong.
He would shake the trees until nuts
rained down on the forest floor.

Squirrel was very fast.
He zipped from nut to nut,
collecting them for supper.

Bear helped Squirrel make a cozy nest of leaves and twigs.

Squirrel helped Bear tidy up his den.

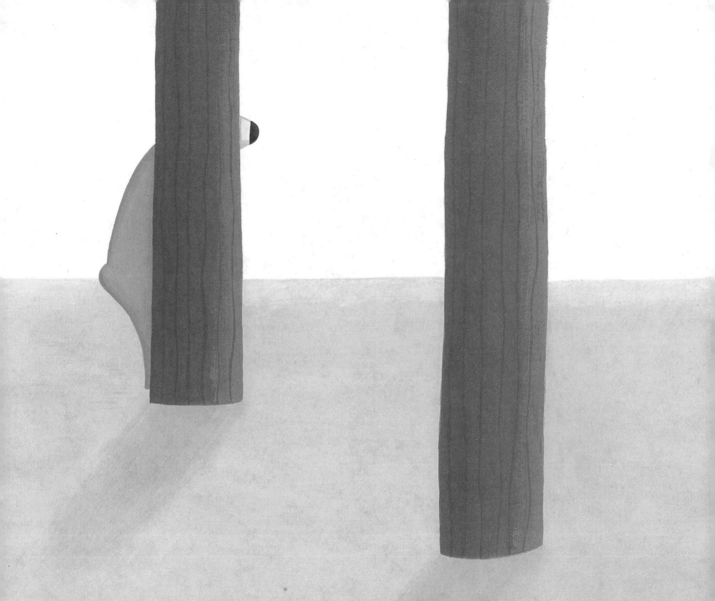

And they both liked to play games.

The other squirrels asked,
"Why are you hanging around with a bear?
He'll eat you up for a midnight snack."
Squirrel said, "Don't be silly!
Bear is my friend."

The other bears said, "Squirrel would
make a good midnight snack!"
Bear said, "That's ridiculous!
Squirrel is my friend."

Squirrel and Bear ignored the
other animals' remarks and
went off to play "Guess That Song."

And when Bear settled in for a long winter nap, Squirrel waited patiently for his friend to wake up.

And waited. . . .

And waited.

Until spring finally arrived.
Bear began to stir.

"It's good to see you," said Squirrel.

"It's good to see you too," said Bear.

"You look different," said Squirrel.

"You look different too," said Bear.

"You look delicious," said Bear.

"Why, thank you, Bear," said Squirrel.

"I mean you look like you would
taste delicious," said Bear.

They looked at each other for a long time.

SNiff
SNiff

"I'm sorry, Squirrel, I can't help myself!" said Bear.

Stop, Bear!

Squirrel is your friend!

gnaw nom
CHEW
MUNCH
CRUNCH
mmmm!

But Bear couldn't stop.

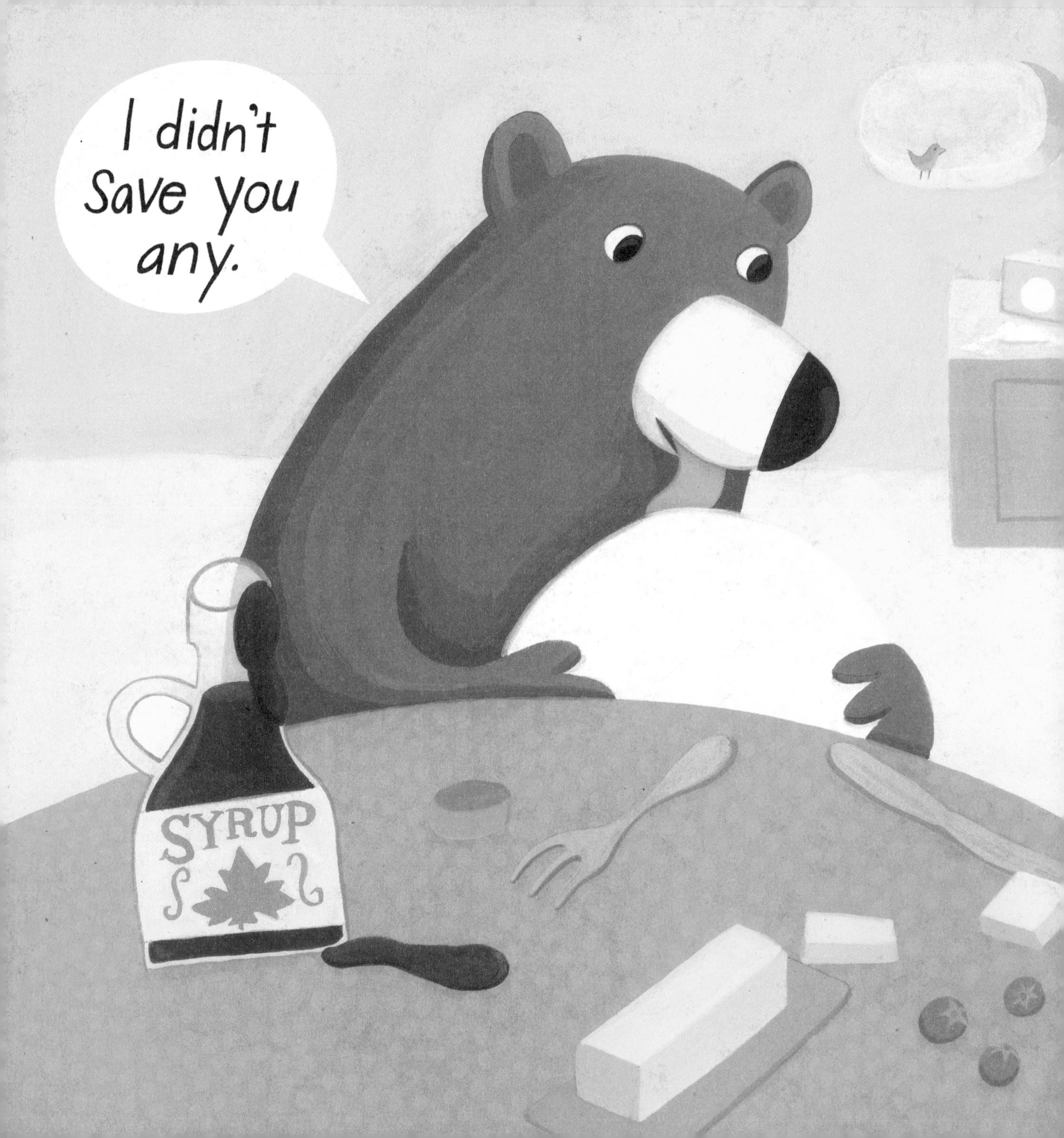
I didn't Save you any.
SYRUP

"It's okay, Bear, I can make more," said Squirrel.

Bear ate all the blueberry pancakes that Squirrel made until not a morsel was left. He ate every last berry. He even licked the plate clean.

But . . .

he did not eat Squirrel.